Pet Shop Follies

Mary Ann Fraser

BOYDS MILLS PRESS

HONESDALE, PENNSYLVANIA

Text and illustrations copyright © 2010 by Mary Ann Fraser

Boyds Mills Press, Inc.
815 Church Street
Honesdale, Pennsylvania 18431
Printed in the United States of America

Library of Congress Cataloging-in-Publication Data

Fraser, Mary Ann.
  Pet shop follies / Mary Ann Fraser. — 1st ed.
    p. cm.
  Summary: No one is coming into the pet shop, so the animals,
from the smallest hamster to the biggest dog, put on a show to
attract customers.
  ISBN 978-1-59078-619-2 (hardcover : alk. paper)
  [1. Pets—Fiction. 2. Stores, Retail—Fiction. 3. Revues—
Fiction.] I. Title.
  PZ7.F86455Peq 2010
  [E]—dc22
                            2009019384

First edition
The text of this book is set in 30-point Optima.
The illustrations are done in gouache.

10 9 8 7 6 5 4 3 2 1

To Cooper, Ainsley, and Jake

No one is coming in.

Let's put on a show!

We need sets,

costumes,

lights,

sound,

and lots of rehearsals.

At last
we are ready.

The curtains open
to reveal . . .

demonstrations of amazing skill

and bravery.

People gather to
hear song

Tap
Tap

Tap   Tap

and dance,

see death-defying stunts

and
surprising
talents.

And after the
grand finale,

everyone comes in
to meet us.

CLOSED
COME AGAIN SOON

E
FRAS

Fraser, Mary Ann.

Pet shop follies.

DATE			